KT-433-794
This book belongs to:

Published by Ladybird Books Ltd
80 Strand London WC2R 0RL
A Penguin Company
17 19 20 18 16

Printed in Italy

The Elves and the Shoemaker

illustrated by Andrew Rowland

Once upon a time, there
was a poor shoemaker
and his wife.

"This is all the leather
I have left," said the poor
shoemaker. "I can make
just one pair of shoes."

That night, the shoemaker cut the leather.

"I'll make these shoes in the morning," he said. He left the leather in the shop and went to bed.

The next morning, the shoemaker came downstairs. To his surprise, the leather had been made into a pair of beautiful shoes.

The shoemaker called his wife.

"Did you make these shoes?"

"No," said his wife, "I didn't make those shoes!"

Just then, a rich lady came into the shop. She picked up the shoes.

"These are the most beautiful shoes I have ever seen," she said.

She gave the shoemaker three gold coins.

With the money, the shoemaker bought some more leather. That night, the shoemaker cut out two pairs of shoes. He left the leather on the table and went to bed.

In the morning, there were two pairs of shoes on the table.

The shoemaker called his wife.

"Did you make these shoes?"

"No," said his wife, "I didn't make those shoes!"

That very morning, a rich man came into the shop.

"What beautiful shoes," said the man. "I must have them. I will pay you six gold coins."

The shoemaker bought some more leather.

“Now I can make three pairs of shoes,” he said.

He worked late into the night cutting the leather. Then he went to bed.

The next morning, the shoemaker came downstairs.

On the table were three pairs of beautiful shoes.

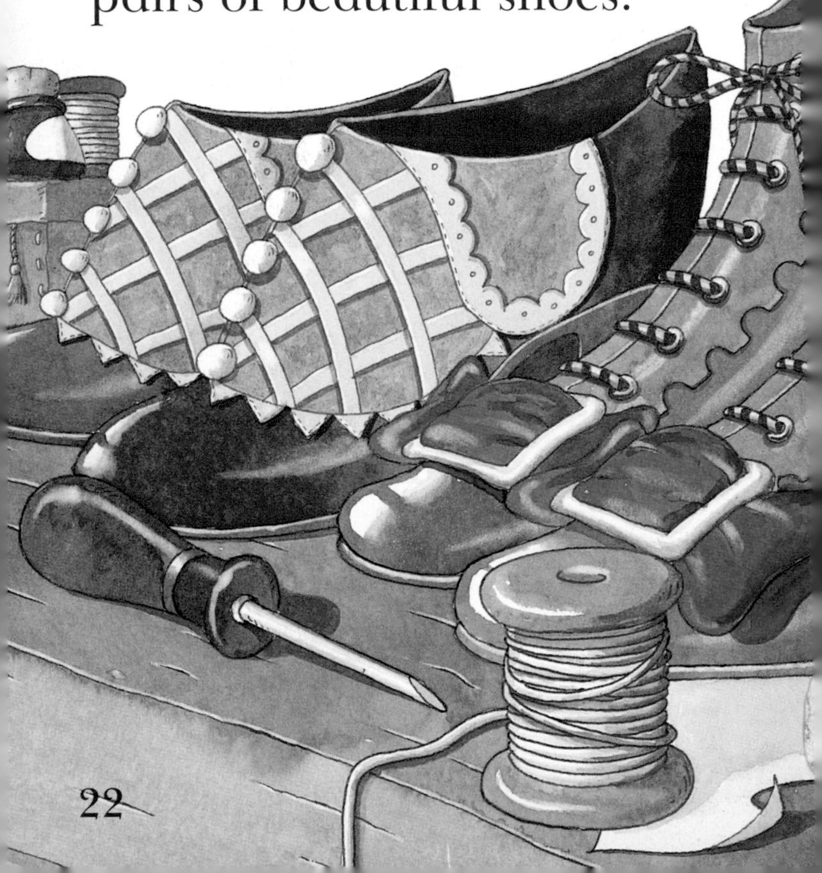

The shoemaker called
his wife.

"We must find out who is
making these beautiful shoes
for us," said the shoemaker.

The next night, the shoemaker worked very hard. He cut the leather for four pairs of shoes. But this time, the shoemaker and his wife hid in the shop.

At midnight, the door of the shop opened and in came two little elves dressed in rags. They jumped up onto the table and opened their little green bags.

The elves stitched and sewed and hammered all night.

By morning, they had made four pairs of shoes. Then they picked up their bags and ran out of the shop.

The shoemaker said to his wife, "The elves have helped us, but how can we help them?"

"I know what we can do!" said his wife.

The shoemaker and his wife worked very hard. They made two pairs of little green shoes, some little green clothes, and two little green hats.

That night, they left the little green shoes, hats and clothes in the shop. Then they hid again.

At midnight, the door of the shop opened and the elves came in.

When they saw the little green shoes, the little green clothes and the little green hats, they were very surprised. They put them on at once.

The little elves went on helping the shoemaker and his wife to make beautiful shoes. And the shoemaker and his wife made more clothes for the little elves.

And the shoemaker and his wife, and the two little elves all lived happily ever after.

Read It Yourself is a series of graded readers designed to give young children a confident and successful start to reading.

Level 3 is suitable for children who are developing reading confidence and stamina, and who are ready to progress to longer stories with a wider vocabulary. The stories are told simply and with a richness of language.

About this book

At this stage of reading development, it's rewarding to ask children how they prefer to approach each new story. Some children like to look first at the pictures and discuss them with an adult. Some children prefer the adult to read the story to them before they attempt it for themselves. Many children at this stage will be eager to read the story aloud to an adult at once, and to discuss it afterwards. Unknown words can be worked out by looking at the beginning letter (*what sound does this letter make?*) and the sounds the child recognises within the word. The child can then decide which word would make sense.

Developing readers need lots of praise and encouragement.